"You'd better watch out," Danny warned. He clicked his teeth together shark-style. "I'm Deadly Danny, Killer Swimmer."

"More like Dog-Paddle Danny," Tonya said with a snicker.

Danny's cheeks burned. "I'm a champion swimmer!"

"Don't you mean a champion *sinker*?"

"You'll see at camp!" Danny shouted.

A slow smile spread across Tonya's face. "*You're* going to Camp Kickapoo?"

Danny stared at her, too scared to blink or even breathe.

Tonya leaned forward until her nose practically touched Danny's. "What's wrong, Deadly Danny? Shark got your tongue?"

For Twig
and
For Emily, Killer Swimmer

Text copyright © 1997 by Gibbs Davis
Illustrations copyright © 1997 by Abby Carter
All rights reserved under International and Pan-American Copyright Conventions.
Published in the United States by Random House, Inc., New York, and simultaneously in Canada by Random House of Canada Limited, Toronto.

http://www.randomhouse.com/

Library of Congress Cataloging-in-Publication Data
Davis, Gibbs.
Camp sink or swim / by Gibbs Davis ; illustrated by Abby Carter.
p. cm. "A Stepping Stone book."
Summary: In trouble at camp because he has bragged about his non-existent swimming abilities, eight-year-old Danny finds himself forming an unexpected alliance with the bully "Two Ton" Tonya.
ISBN 0-679-88216-2 (trade). — ISBN 0-679-98216-7 (lib. bdg.)
[1. Camps — Fiction. 2. Swimming — Fiction. 3. Bullies — Fiction.
4. Friendship — Fiction.] I. Carter, Abby, ill. II. Title. PZ7.D2886Cam 1997
[Fic] — dc21 96-50356

Printed in the United States of America 10 9 8 7 6 5 4 3 2 1

Camp Sink
or
Swim

by Gibbs Davis

illustrated by Abby Carter

A STEPPING STONE BOOK

RANDOM HOUSE 🏠 NEW YORK

[1]

Big Mouth Biggs

"Danny Biggs, you're a liar!"

Tonya Wallace stomped through the lawn sprinkler. Her pudgy hands were balled into fists. She was headed straight for Danny's yard.

"Run!" Danny yelled to his best friend, Billy Webb. "Two Ton Tonya's coming!"

It was too late. Tonya's huge shadow covered both boys. Water ran down her angry face.

"Big Mouth Biggs, you never caught a hundred-pound killer fish!" Tonya shouted so the whole neighborhood could hear. "You just lied to wreck my Camp Kickapoo record. You're a big fat liar!"

"Ha-ha-hick." Danny's nervous laugh turned into a hiccup.

Billy shoved his face in Tonya's. "Look

who's talking about being big and fa—"

Before Billy could finish, Tonya knocked him down and sat on him.

Billy's arms and legs kicked the air. But he didn't move an inch. "Quick, Danny, tell her how you caught Old Ralph!"

A handful of neighborhood kids stopped to listen. It was only two weeks into summer, but everyone was already bored. Danny lit up inside. He loved having an audience. He sat down on the grass and began his story.

"Old Ralph had been swimming in the Tomahawk River for a hundred years. Every year that old musky got fatter and fatter."

Whoops. Danny shot a look at Tonya. Maybe he should have skipped the fat part.

Tonya crossed her arms. "Go on."

Danny took a deep breath and continued. "Last summer, Old Ralph tipped over a boat full of tourists. He ate a whole family, shoes and everything."

Tonya narrowed her eyes at him. "Muskies don't live a hundred years, and they don't eat shoes."

Everyone waited for Danny's answer.

Danny tugged at his chewed-up shoe-laces. He knew if he didn't think of something good, Tonya would sit on him, too.

Suddenly, Danny pointed at his shoes. "These shoelaces are proof! They were hanging out of Old Ralph's mouth after he ate the last tourist."

Everyone leaned forward to see.

Tonya shook her head. "Anyone can have old shoelaces."

"Tell her how you caught him," Billy whispered.

Danny looked at his friend. Billy lay as flat as a pancake under Tonya. He wasn't even kicking anymore. Danny knew he had to make this story really good.

"First I swam the river so Old Ralph would get used to me," Danny said.

"Wasn't the current too strong?" asked a boy in swimming trunks.

"Not for me," said Danny. "I'm a champion swimmer. I can swim a mile upstream without stopping."

Everyone looked impressed—except Tonya. Danny quickly went on with his story.

"Every day Old Ralph swam a little closer, until one day we were swimming eyeball to eyeball. That's when I hypnotized him like this." Danny rolled his eyes from side to side to demonstrate. "That old musky followed me right onto the shore. We cooked

him up for supper. *De-e-e-licious*."

The kids laughed when Danny rubbed his stomach and licked his lips.

Tonya narrowed her eyes into slits. "Liar. You can't hypnotize fish. I want *real* proof."

"Help," Billy squeaked beneath Tonya.

Danny had to think fast. "I've got Old Ralph's teeth in a jar at home."

"Okay, Big Mouth. Let's go see." Tonya slowly stood up.

Billy rolled over and gasped for air. He smiled up at Danny. "Thanks, buddy. You saved my life."

A couple of kids patted Danny's back.

Then Billy leaned forward and whispered, "Do you *really* have Old Ralph's teeth?"

Danny froze. His story had sounded so real, he had almost believed it himself. What was he going to show Tonya? All he had was an old baby tooth in a peanut butter jar.

Tonya gave Danny a shove. "Let's go, Biggs. It's tooth time."

I'm dead, thought Danny. *Tonya will kill me when she sees my dumb little baby tooth.*

Danny had no choice. He slowly led everyone into his backyard.

Mrs. Biggs stopped Danny at the back door. "Sorry, kids, but it's almost dinnertime. You'd all better go home. Danny will see you tomorrow."

Danny had never been so happy to see his mother in his whole life. He flung open the screen door and hugged her.

"Later, Dan my man!" Billy said.

"Chill, Bill!" Danny waved as everyone left his yard—except Tonya.

Tonya pressed her nose against the screen and whispered, "I'll see you tomorrow morning. And you'd better not be lying."

"See ya." Danny slammed the door shut.

"You look upset, honey," said Mrs. Biggs. "Are you still sad about Billy leaving for Camp Kickapoo this Friday?"

Camp Kickapoo! How could he have forgotten? Tonya was leaving for camp this Friday, too. All he had to do was hide inside for the next few days until everyone left for camp! By the time they returned, Tonya wouldn't even remember the teeth.

Mrs. Biggs smiled. "I have a big treat for you after dinner tonight."

That could only mean one thing—brownies and ice cream. Danny smiled as he ran up the stairs, two at a time. What a day! He had saved his best friend's life and escaped Tonya, *and* his mom had made his favorite dessert!

Later that evening, Danny snuggled under the covers and waited for his parents to come in and say good night. His stomach was stuffed with brownies and ice cream.

"That's it!" he said. A stomachache was the perfect excuse for staying inside until Friday. *I'm brilliant*, he thought.

Mr. and Mrs. Biggs came into Danny's bedroom. When Mrs. Biggs sat on his bed, Danny made his best sick face for her.

"Are you feeling okay?" she asked, and pressed her cool hand against his forehead.

"Danny'll feel just fine after he hears our surprise," said Mr. Biggs.

"Ready for your treat?" asked Mrs. Biggs.

Danny's eyes widened. "*More* brownies?"

Mrs. Biggs laughed and shook her head. "Your Dad and I know how much you wanted to go to Camp Kickapoo with Billy last summer. You're almost nine now. We've decided that's old enough to be away from home for a little while."

Mr. Biggs held out a sweatshirt. CAMP KICKAPOO was printed across the front. Beneath it was a picture of a kangaroo. "You're all signed up, sport. This Friday you'll be on the bus to camp with your friends."

Danny's mouth dropped open.

"I knew he'd be surprised." Mrs. Biggs kissed Danny's cheek and got up to leave.

"Wait!" shouted Danny. "I don't want to go to camp!"

Mr. Biggs tousled Danny's hair. "It's always a little rough your first time away from home, sport. After a couple of days you'll love it. Take it from an old ex-camper."

"Sweet dreams." Mrs. Biggs pulled up Danny's covers and turned off the bedside light. Mr. Biggs closed the door.

Danny collapsed back on his pillow. He reached under his bed for the peanut butter jar. Inside it was a tiny tooth. "I can't show this to Tonya. It won't even pass for a *baby* killer-fish tooth."

Danny thought hard. Maybe Tonya wouldn't expect him to take Old Ralph's teeth to camp. Real killer-fish teeth were much too valuable to risk losing. That made sense. Even Tonya might buy that.

Danny slipped on the Camp Kickapoo sweatshirt. He felt like a real camper already. Billy had told him about all the fun things he'd done at camp last summer—hikes, cookouts, campfires, making cool crafts, and lots of swimming in Kickapoo Lake.

Danny sat up. His heart was pounding. Today he had told everyone he was a champion swimmer. Even Billy had believed him. There was just one little problem. He whispered his secret to the goofy-looking kangaroo on his Camp Kickapoo sweatshirt.

"I can't swim."

[2]

Deadly Danny, Killer Swimmer and Champion Sinker

"Help! I'm drowning!"

Danny opened his eyes and sighed with relief. It was just a dream. He shuddered as he remembered it.

Tonya had forced him into a boat and rowed to the middle of Lake Kickapoo. "Okay, Big Mouth," she said. "Let's see you swim now." Then she shoved him overboard.

A killer fish was about to eat him. That's when he woke up.

Danny shuffled into the bathroom. He stared at himself in the mirror. "I'm a dead man," he said.

"Danny, breakfast!" his mother called.

Danny found his mother downstairs at the kitchen table. She was sewing name tags on all his summer clothes. "'Morning, sleepyhead." She pointed to a stack of

14

pancakes. "Help yourself," she told him.

Danny took a pancake and poked holes in it with his fork. How was he going to tell his mother he was a coward?

"What's wrong, honey?"

Danny blinked hard, trying to work up some tears. "I can't swim, and there's a big bully at camp who wants to drown me." He paused to sniffle in his napkin. His mother leaned forward. She looked concerned.

Good, thought Danny. *It's working.* "Mom, please don't make me go."

"Don't worry, honey. The camp counselors won't let anyone hurt you."

"She'll drown me in the lake!"

"No one's going to drown you, Danny. And do you know why?"

Danny looked up at his mother, hopeful. "Because I'm not going to camp?"

"No. Because you're going to learn to swim at camp."

"But, Mom—"

Mrs. Biggs held up a hand to silence him. "I don't want to hear another word. Now get dressed, because we're going shopping."

"Shopping for what?"

"To buy you a swimsuit."

"Danny! Do you want me to come in and help you?" Mrs. Biggs shouted across the Boys' Department.

"No! Stay out!" Why did his mother always have to embarrass him when they went shopping?

Danny stood on a pile of cutesy swim-suits his mother had selected. He wouldn't be caught dead in any of them. There was just one left. The only one he had picked out himself. He pulled it on and let the elastic waistband snap against his stomach. Good fit.

"Now for the real test," said Danny. How cool did he look? He checked himself out in the mirror. Two skinny legs poked out from under baggy swim trunks covered with jagged-toothed sharks.

"Way cool," Danny said, flexing his arms. "I'm Deadly Danny, Killer Swimmer." He admired himself from every angle. Then he

quickly dressed and gave the trunks to his
mother at the cash register.

"Don't wander too far," said Mrs. Biggs.
But Danny disappeared into the next department.

"Oops." Danny bumped into a rack of
clothes. A big pink swimsuit fell onto his
head. He examined the daisy-covered suit.

"It's a *girl's*," he realized with disgust.

Danny stretched the suit like a rubber band and let it go. It soared high and landed on a girl's back.

"Bull's-eye." Danny quickly hid behind some bathrobes. The girl turned around, searching for the culprit.

A chill shot up Danny's back as he recognized the face. "Two Ton Tonya," he whispered. Then he noticed a sign on the wall above her head: BIG GIRLS.

"The fatso department," he whispered with delight. This was too good to be true. He wished Billy was here. It was easier to make fun of someone with a buddy.

He watched Tonya pick up the pink swimsuit and step into a dressing room.

"Hurry up, honeybun," said a large woman who could only be Tonya's mother.

Finally, Tonya's chubby face reappeared. She checked to see if the coast was clear and tiptoed out. Her arms and legs bulged out from the skin-tight pink suit. Daisies circled her round tummy. She stood in front of a full-length mirror, looking miserable.

"We have some lovely beach cover-ups," a saleslady suggested.

"It's pink, your favorite color," said Tonya's mother, trying hard to be cheerful. "I think you look very pretty."

Tonya pulled away. "I do not. I look fat."

Fat? She looks like a whale, Danny thought. He had to stuff a fist in his mouth to keep from laughing out loud.

When Tonya started back toward the dressing room, Danny stepped forward. "Hi, Tonya!" he said in his loudest voice. "Nice suit."

Tonya froze.

"Say 'thank you,' honeybun," said her mother.

Tonya slowly turned around. Her face matched the bright pink of her swimsuit. "Go away, Biggs," she whispered.

Just then, Danny's mother found him. "Danny, there you are!"

Danny reached into his mother's shopping bag for his new swimsuit. He dangled it in front of Tonya. "I'm Deadly Danny, Killer

Swimmer. Better watch out," he said. Then he clicked his teeth together shark-style.

"More like Dog-Paddle Danny," Tonya said with a snicker.

Danny's cheeks burned. "I'm a champion swimmer!"

"Don't you mean a champion *sinker?*"

"You'll see at camp!" Danny shouted.

A slow smile spread across Tonya's face. "*You're* going to Camp Kickapoo?"

Danny stared at her.

Tonya leaned forward until her nose practically touched Danny's. "What's wrong, Deadly Danny? Shark got your tongue?"

Danny took his mother by the hand and pulled. "We've got to go. Bye!"

"Bye-bye," Tonya said sweetly. "See you in the water, Danny!" Then she clicked her teeth together shark-style.

"Is Tonya going to camp, too?" asked Mrs. Biggs.

Danny didn't answer. He was too busy imagining all the ways Tonya could drown him at Camp Kickapoo.

[3]

Crash Course with Killer Bubbles

Danny couldn't keep his secret to himself one second longer. That afternoon he invited Billy over and spilled the beans.

"I can't swim," Danny confessed. "I can't even float."

Billy laughed. "Pretty funny, Dan my man."

Danny didn't crack a smile.

Finally, Billy realized he wasn't joking. "Tonya's going to kill you," he said, "unless…"

Danny was desperate. He grabbed Billy and shook him. "Unless *what?*"

"Unless you learn to swim before camp starts."

"In two days?" Danny asked. "You mean a crash course?"

Billy nodded. "Wish I could help you, but I only know how to hold my breath in the tub. I got a bad cold last summer and the camp nurse wouldn't let me go in the lake."

Just then, Mrs. Webb shouted from across the street. "Billy! You promised to clean the garage today!"

Billy groaned. "Sorry, Danny. Gotta go."

Danny watched his friend cross the street. He had never felt more alone. How could he learn to swim in two days? His parents would be no help. The closest his dad came to water was the lawn sprinkler. And his mom hated getting wet. She practically wore a shower cap to brush her teeth!

Danny's gaze turned up the street and stopped at the Lime Rock Library. *Maybe I can read a book on how to swim*, Danny thought. It was worth a try.

He quickly biked to the library and burst through the doors. "Where's the—"

"Sh-h-h-h!" A woman behind the front desk pointed to a QUIET PLEASE sign.

Danny tiptoed up to her. He saw she was wearing dangly fish earrings.

It's a sign, he thought. *I'm saved.*

"I have to learn to swim in two days," he blurted. "Can you help me?"

The librarian's fishy earrings swung back and forth as she shook her head. "Nobody learns to swim in just two days. Maybe you should sign up for lessons at the YMCA. In the meantime, I'll help you get started."

She showed him a book with pictures of different swimming strokes. "Check our video section, too," she suggested, pointing the way.

When he got there, Danny found a video titled *Basics of Swimming*. "Bor-r-r-ring," he said, putting it back. Then he spotted a movie with a dolphin on the cover.

He read the title. "*Flipper*. Perfect!" After all, who could swim better than a dolphin? They *lived* in the water.

Danny checked out the book and movie and headed for his next stop, Patsy's Pets.

The pet store was filled with caged puppies and kittens. Danny walked past them to the fish tanks in back. He watched a bowl of goldfish for a long time.

"I can do that," he said, shaping his

mouth into a big O. He opened and closed it like a fish. Then he flapped his arms up and down by his sides like fins.

Finally, Patsy asked him, "Are you going to buy a fish or just act like one?"

Danny pointed to the smallest goldfish. "How much?"

"That runt? A buck, and I'll even throw in some free fish flakes."

Danny pulled a wrinkled dollar bill out of his pocket. "It's a deal."

He watched Patsy scoop his goldfish out of the tank and drop it into a plastic baggie filled with water.

"What will you name it?" Patsy asked.

"I don't know yet."

Danny carefully laid the baggie in his bike basket and pushed off. By the time he was home he had thought of the perfect name.

"I'm calling you Killer Bubbles," he said.

He found a glass bowl for his fish, and that night they watched *Flipper* together. Then Danny took his library book into the bathtub to try some swimming strokes.

Suddenly, there was a rap on the bathroom door. "Danny! Tonya phoned!" called his mother. "She said she'd save you a seat on the bus to camp! Isn't that nice?"

Danny dropped his book in the bathwater.

"You've been in there for over an hour! Are you okay?"

"I'm fine! Go away!" By the time Danny fished out the book, most of the bathwater was on the floor. It took six towels to soak it all up. And he still didn't know how to swim.

Time was running out. He needed help.

Danny tapped on the fish bowl. "What am I gonna do, Killer?" But Killer Bubbles was too busy gobbling fish flakes to care.

The next morning, Danny saw water everywhere he looked: the sink, the toilet, the lawn sprinkler, even the ice cube trays.

Camp was one day away. He needed a plan! Suddenly, the librarian's words ran through his mind. *You should sign up for swimming lessons at the YMCA.*

"That's it!" he cried.

Danny picked up Billy and they bicycled over to the YMCA together. As they walked inside, Billy pinched his nose and made a face. "Chlorine," he said.

They followed the strong smell to the Pool Room and found a lifeguard sitting on a chair high above the pool.

"Can you teach me to swim in one day?" Danny asked.

The lifeguard nearly fell off her chair laughing. "If you're a dolphin," she said. "Otherwise, it takes weeks of lessons and practice."

¤ ¤ ¤

At dinner that night, Danny couldn't eat. In his mind, his fish sticks had turned into pet goldfish. And Tonya kept trying to bite off their heads.

"I know what will pick up your appetite." Mr. Biggs set a big atlas on the dinner table. He pointed to a map of Minnesota. "This is where you're going to camp."

"What are all those blue spots?" Danny asked. The map was covered with them.

"Lakes," said Mr. Biggs.

Danny nearly choked on a cherry tomato. "But there are *hundreds* of them!"

"Thousands," corrected Mr. Biggs. "Minnesota is called the Land of 10,000 Lakes. Camp Kickapoo is right here on Kickapoo Lake." He pointed to a blue dot.

Danny gulped. With all that *water* around, Tonya was sure to drown him.

"I can't go to camp!" he shouted. "I'm not even packed!"

"I've taken care of all that," said his mother. "Here's the list the camp sent us.

Everything's in your duffel bag, ready to go."

Danny squirmed as he read the list:

insect repellent
mosquito netting
flashlight
rain poncho...

Danny felt itchy and wet just reading it. Where *was* this place? The jungle?

He looked at his parents with suspicion. Maybe they were sick and tired of their son. Maybe they were sending him to camp *hoping* he'd drown or get eaten by bugs!

Mr. Biggs gave Danny a good-night hug. "Better turn in, sport. The camp bus leaves bright and early tomorrow."

Danny dragged himself upstairs and got ready for bed. As he slid under the covers, he imagined all the ways Tonya could drown him in the Land of 10,000 Lakes.

"If only I had a bad cold, like Billy did last summer," Danny said. "Then the camp nurse wouldn't even let me go in the water."

Danny sat up in bed. "That's it!"

He'd call Billy first thing in the morning.

[4]

Welcome to Camp Kickapoo!

The following morning, Danny and Billy got in line to board the Camp Kickapoo bus.

"Did you bring everything?" Billy whispered.

Danny opened his duffel bag. On top lay his Tonya Survival Kit—sneezing powder, a tube of fake boogers from a novelty store, an onion, Kleenex, and his mom's red lipstick.

Suddenly, someone knocked on a bus window to get his attention. Inside the bus, a horrible face was smashed against the glass.

"It's Tonya," he whispered with a shiver. "She's going to get me. I can't do this."

"Yes, you can," Billy said. "Stick to the plan."

Danny pulled out the red lipstick and rubbed some on his nose.

Billy nodded. "You look sick as a dog."

Danny took a deep breath and slowly climbed the bus steps. Tonya was waiting for him. She grinned and patted the empty seat beside her. "I saved it just for you."

"No, thanks," Danny said, moving along.

"Hold it, Biggs." Tonya stuck out her arm and he bumped into it. "Nice nose, Bozo. But this bus goes to camp, not the circus."

Danny froze as a few kids laughed.

Billy whispered to Danny. "Do it."

"I've got a bad cold," Danny said, reaching inside his duffel bag. He squeezed some of the fake boogers into his hand and raised it to his face. Then he pretended to sneeze.

"Ah-ah-ah-ah-CHOO!"

Fake boogers sprayed all over Tonya's face and hair. She gasped in horror.

Danny and Billy hurried to the back of the bus and slipped into a seat. Billy gave Danny a high-five. "Told you it would work. Fake boogers never fail. Gross-out guaranteed!"

Danny gave his duffel a pat. He hoped Billy was right. He was depending on his bag of tricks to keep him out of the water.

Suddenly, Tonya stood and shouted across the bus, "We're not finished yet, Biggs!"

Her voice sent a chill up Danny's back.

The bus driver turned around. "That's it! Not another peep out of you!" he ordered.

Hours later, they finally arrived at Camp Kickapoo. A big man with a bushy beard greeted them as they got off the bus.

"Welcome, boys and girls! I'm Mr. Mike, your camp director. This is Luther, our camp dog," he said, patting a big, happy mutt with sandy fur the same color as Mr. Mike's beard.

"And these are your counselors." Mr. Mike

pointed to a dozen scruffy-looking teenagers in T-shirts, baggy shorts, and baseball caps.

"Think of your counselor as a big brother or sister," said Mr. Mike. "They're here to help you. Each camper will be assigned to a tent with five other kids and a counselor. Now, let's divide up. Boys on my right for North Camp and girls on my left for South Camp."

Danny tugged on Billy's sleeve. "Did you hear that? We're separated from the girls! Tonya won't be anywhere near me!"

Billy clapped him on the back. "Told you everything would work out."

Tonya glared at Danny as she crossed over to the girls' side.

A tall, red-headed teenage boy with freckles stepped forward. "I'm Pete, the head counselor. I know you're all pooped after the long ride, so let's get to your bunks before dinner. Raise your hand when I call your name. I'll tell you your tent and counselor."

Billy whispered, "The boys' tents have fish names."

Danny crossed his fingers behind his

back. "Shark, shark, shark." He whispered his wish three times for good luck.

Billy was assigned to Pete's tent right away.

"Put it there, Wild Bill," Pete said, holding out his hand, palm up. Billy slapped it as though they were already old pals.

Pete read through the list of names until only Danny and a handful of boys were left. Danny felt left out as he watched Billy kid around with his new bunkmates. Had they forgotten to put his name on the list?

Finally, Pete called, "Danny Biggs!"

Danny's hand shot up. "Here I am! I'm here!" he shouted.

Pete grinned. "Bet you thought we forgot all about you. You're in my tent with your buddy Billy. We like to keep friends together their first year at camp."

Danny couldn't stop smiling. Tonya was going to be too far away to drown him, *and* he got to bunk with his best friend. He dragged his duffel bag over to Billy.

Pete passed out maps of Camp Kickapoo.

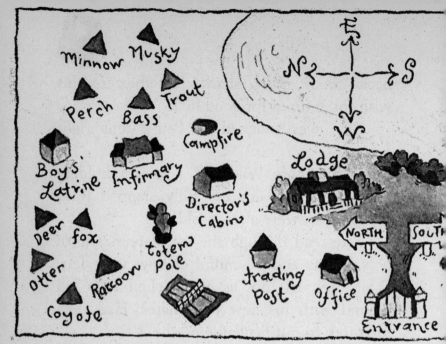

"These will help you find your way around. In a few days, this'll feel like home and you won't need them."

Pete gave them a salute. "This way to North Camp, men! Form a line and follow me!" He did a military goose-step, lifting his legs high until everyone was laughing. He led them past the parking lot and through the camp's main gate. They stopped at a fork in the road.

Two signs pointed in opposite directions. One arrow pointed toward North Camp, and

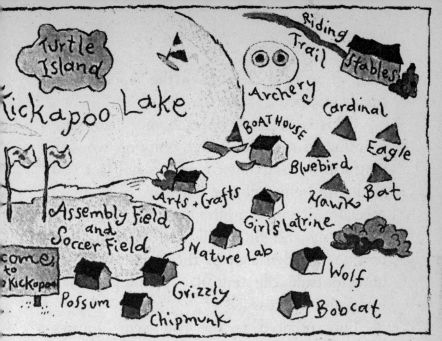

the other pointed toward South Camp.

"This is where we separate the boys from the girls," Pete said. "So which way do we want to go, men?"

"North!"

Pete pretended to be blown backward by the force of their answer. "You guys don't know your own strength."

Danny felt a thrill as he and his fellow campers grinned at each other. They followed Pete past the Main Lodge and around a big totem pole carved like a giant bird. When they came to a clearing in the woods, they finally stopped.

"This is it, home sweet home," Pete said, pointing to a circle of five tents on wooden platforms. "Your tent counselors will get you settled in before dinner. Then we're having a special welcome campfire down by the lake."

Danny and Billy followed Pete to their tent. A wooden sign in the shape of a fish hung outside the tent flap opening. MUSKY was painted across it.

Billy pointed to the fish sign. "I can't believe it! We're in Musky!"

"It's almost as good as Shark," Danny agreed. He was glad they weren't in the Minnow tent next to them.

Pete walked up behind them. "Are you two fishermen?"

"Kind of," Billy said, turning shy.

"Sure we are," Danny bragged. He started telling Pete about catching Old Ralph.

"Sounds like a good campfire story," Pete said. "Save it for later. Right now we've got to choose bunks and bunkmates."

Danny and Billy raced to the closest bunk bed, in the front of the tent. "Top!" Danny shouted. "Bottom!" Billy cried.

After everyone put away their clothes, Pete asked the boys to sit on their bunks. Then he pulled a small tree branch out.

"This is a talking stick," he explained. "Whoever holds it is the only one who gets to talk. No interrupting. Let's pass it around and get to know each other. Say something about where you're from and what you like to do."

Pete held up the stick. "I'll start. I'm eighteen and I'm from Wisconsin. I've been coming to Camp Kickapoo since I was your age. My best friends were all my bunkmates. And I'll bet that the other boys here in Musky will become *your* best friends, too."

Pete handed the talking stick to a pudgy boy munching potato chips. "My name's Noah," he said. "My Mom said I can go home if I don't like it here. I like computer games."

Noah's bunkmate was hanging upside down over the top bunk watching him. The bunkmate's glasses slid off his face, but Noah reached out and caught them before they hit the ground. Noah handed the glasses and the talking stick up to his bunkmate.

"Thanks." The small boy sat up, his cowboy boots sticking over the edge of the bed. He peered at them through his glasses.

"My name's Sam, but my nickname's Tex, 'cuz I'm from Texas. I've got a horse named Sailor. See?" He pulled a photo from his pocket and held it up. Everyone leaned forward, even though it was too far away to see.

Matt and Jimmy were next. They were identical twins from Iowa. Danny recognized them from the bus ride.

Danny could barely keep still waiting for his turn. Talking about himself was his favorite thing in the world. When the twins finished, he reached out and grabbed the talking stick from Matt.

"I'm Danny Biggs!" he announced in a loud voice. "I'm from Iowa, too!"

Then something happened to Danny that had never happened before. His mind went blank. He couldn't think of anything more to say. Everyone started to look bored.

Pete nodded toward Billy. Danny knew Pete wanted him to pass the stick, but he couldn't. He felt as though he was going to explode. "I caught a killer musky once!" he blurted.

Noah put down his chips. Tex's eyes widened. Matt and Jimmy stopped breathing.

Danny went on. "And I'm also a champion swimmer."

"Very impressive," Pete said, lifting the stick from his hand. "But we have to stop. It's time for dinner. Anyone hungry?"

"I could eat a horse," said Noah.

Tex frowned until his glasses slid down his face. "Not my horse, you don't!"

Pete had the boys use their maps to find the Mess Hall in the Main Lodge. "Good teamwork," he said when they got there. "This is where you'll be eating your meals."

Danny looked up from his map and saw a stream of girls going inside. Girls? *This can't be the place*, he thought. But MESS HALL was carved above the door. What was going on?

Danny ran up to Pete for an explanation. "I thought the girls stayed in South Camp."

"They do," Pete said. "Except for meals. Girls have to eat, too, you know."

Billy whispered in Danny's ear. "Don't worry. Tonya can't drown you at dinner …unless it's in a bowl of soup."

Danny forced a laugh.

"Meals and swimming are the only times we see the girls," Pete added. "Otherwise it's just us guys."

Danny's feet froze to the ground. "Swimming?"

"There's only one lake," Pete said. "Boys and girls have swimming together every day. You ought to like that."

"Huh?" Danny gave him a blank look.

"Don't be modest," Pete said, clapping him on the back. "You're a champion swimmer, remember?"

Danny nodded weakly as he watched Pete go inside the Mess Hall.

Billy slapped a Kleenex in Danny's hand. "Better start blowing, buddy."

Inside the Mess Hall, Danny was relieved to find boys and girls eating on opposite sides. Danny took his tray through the food line and joined his tentmates at a nearby table.

Noah set down his tray next to Danny. Double helpings of hot dogs, baked beans, and cookies in the shape of kangaroos spilled over his plate. He gave Danny a nudge. "Hey, Danny, your girlfriend wants you."

"Very funny," Danny said, taking a bite of his hot dog.

"He's not kidding. Look." Billy nodded toward the girls' side of the Mess Hall.

Tonya was waving at Danny. When he looked her way, she held up a kangaroo cookie. Then she bit off its head.

Danny started choking on his hot dog.

Noah slapped him on the back. "I don't blame you for getting choked up. She's kind of cute."

Tex peered at Danny through his glasses. "What's wrong with Danny?" he asked.

Billy shook his head. "He doesn't think he has long to live."

[5]

Two Ton Tonya

"Rise and shine, Muskies!" Pete called, rolling up the tent flap. He tossed a daily camp schedule on each bunk.

It was boiling hot inside the tent. Danny kicked off his blanket. Then he smiled, remembering last night's campfire.

After he had told his story about Old Ralph, everyone had clapped and cheered. They hadn't done that for anyone else's story, not even the counselors'.

Dad was right, he thought. *Camp is fun.*

He sat up, dangled his feet over the top bunk, and glanced at his schedule.

DAILY SCHEDULE

• • • • • • • • • • • • • • • • • • •

8:00 breakfast

9:10-10:00 swimming

10:10-11:00 arts & crafts

11:00-12:00 free time

12:15 lunch

1:00–2:00 rest hour

2:00–3:00 horseback riding

3:10–4:00 nature

4:00–5:00 free time

5:30 dinner

7:00 evening program

• • • • • • • • • • • • • • • • • • •

Billy gave Danny's foot a tug. "Look what's after breakfast."

Danny saw the dreaded word. Swimming.

"Come on," Billy whispered as he pulled out the Tonya Survival Kit.

Danny jumped off the top bunk and ran with Billy to the latrine. Once inside, they got to work.

First Billy put a little red lipstick on a tissue and used it to make Danny's face turn a feverish pink. Then Danny cut up an onion. In seconds, his eyes were watering.

"How do I look?" Danny asked.

Billy dabbed some fake boogers under his

nose for the finishing touch. "Perfect."

Armed with Kleenex, Danny headed for the infirmary. His eyes were watering so much he tripped going up the cabin steps.

A woman in a white jacket opened the screen door. "I'm Nurse Mudge," she said. "Looks like you're not feeling well. Come inside."

"I've got a mad gold," Danny said, trying his best to sound stuffed up.

"You mean a bad cold?" she guessed.

Danny nodded and gave a little moan.

Nurse Mudge put a hand on his forehead. "That's funny, you look feverish but don't feel warm."

She placed a thermometer under Danny's tongue. "Stay still, I'll fill out your chart."

As soon as Nurse Mudge left the room, Danny looked for a way to heat up the thermometer. He was about to give up when he noticed the table lamp beside him.

"That's it," he whispered. He quickly held the thermometer over the light bulb and watched the mercury inside slowly rise.

"Time's up," Nurse Mudge said, returning.

Danny barely had time to pop the thermometer back into his mouth.

Nurse Mudge read the thermometer. "Hmm. You have a slight fever. Would you like to stay here and rest in bed today?"

The thought of being stuck inside on such a hot day sounded like torture. "No way," Danny said. "I mean, no thanks. I just don't think I should go swimming."

Danny was about to start begging when he saw Nurse Mudge already writing a note that would excuse him from swimming.

After breakfast, Danny showed the note to his camp counselor.

"I don't get it," Pete said. "You didn't have a cold last night."

Danny shrugged and dabbed his nose.

"Too bad you'll miss swimming your first week at camp. Listen, why don't you put on your swimsuit and come watch? It's much cooler by the lake. What do you say?"

"Sure!" Danny couldn't wait to show off his new swimsuit with the sharks. This was perfect. He got to be a big shot without ever having to go in the water.

The Muskies changed into their swimsuits and joined the other boys.

"Come on, you monkeys!" Pete shouted, leading the way. "That cold water's waiting!"

Danny flung a towel over his shoulder and ran after him. As they approached the lake, he heard the sounds of kids splashing and shouting. His eyes opened wide as the clear blue of Kickapoo Lake came into sight.

Dozens of boys and girls were jumping off the dock, swimming, sailing, and canoeing. For an instant, Danny forgot all about Tonya.

One of the boys yelled "Charge!" and everyone ran down to the shore.

They almost made it to the water when a muscular man in a swimsuit stepped in front of them. He held up a hand like a stop sign and blew a whistle hanging around his neck.

Danny stopped so suddenly that Billy crashed right into him.

"Rule number one," the man said. "There will be no running on my waterfront."

"Who's he?" Danny whispered to Pete.

"I'm Cutter Shear, the Waterfront Director," the man said, lifting his sunglasses to stare directly at Danny.

Danny grinned sheepishly.

"Now follow me," Cutter continued. "The girls are waiting for us."

"Oh, no, Tonya alert." Billy pointed straight ahead to a dozen girls sitting on the pier. The largest girl in a bright pink swimsuit was looking Danny's way.

Danny recognized her instantly. Two Ton Tonya. Suddenly he couldn't move.

"You're safe," Billy whispered. "The nurse's note, remember?"

Danny took a deep breath. Billy was right. *What am I afraid of? I'm Deadly Danny,* he thought. *She can't hurt me.*

But before his foot hit the pier, Tonya pointed at him and shouted, "Hey, here comes Dog-Paddle Danny!"

All the girls turned to look.

Danny's mouth dropped open, but nothing came out. Billy quickly stepped forward to cover for him. "You're just jealous! 'Jaws' Biggs here could outswim you any day!"

"Yeah," all the boys agreed.

Tonya snickered. "*Jaws?* Big Mouth Biggs is more like it."

A girl spoke to Tonya. "Good one, Twig."

Tonya whispered something to the other girls, and they all giggled.

Danny's cheeks felt like red-hot coals. He couldn't let her get away with embarrassing him in front of his bunkmates. He stepped up, coming face to face with Tonya.

"You're 'Twig'?" he said, forcing a laugh. "What's that? Some cutesy camp name?"

"All the girls have camp names," Tonya said, turning her back on him.

Danny was almost sure he heard her whisper "Dog-Paddle Danny" as the girls burst into peals of laughter. His ears burned. He had to get back at her. But how?

Suddenly, it came to him. The perfect revenge. He walked past Tonya to a girl with long black braids. "Hey, want to know Tonya's nickname back in Iowa?"

The girl looked at him with mild interest.

"Don't," Tonya whispered to Danny. Her voice was pleading.

The look on her face made Danny feel powerful. "Two Ton Tonya!" he shouted. "That's her *real* nickname."

Some of the boys snickered. A few girls giggled behind Tonya's back.

Red-faced, Tonya wrapped her beach towel around herself and looked across the lake. She waved halfheartedly at some kids in a canoe. No one waved back.

She looked so miserable Danny almost felt sorry for her. But then he remembered all the times back home when she had scared him from his own front yard. This was his chance to get even.

"Tonya, you have such a pretty chin," Danny said loudly. "Is that why you decided to add two more?"

Billy and the other boys started laughing. Even some of the girls laughed. Danny felt unbeatable. He was on a roll.

"They say travel broadens a person," he

said, pausing for the punchline. "Looks like you've been all over the world!"

Everyone was still laughing when Cutter walked back onto the dock carrying an armful of life jackets. "I'm glad to see you kids all getting along so well. Now, what do you say we make like fish and learn to swim?"

Most of the kids nodded enthusiastically. Danny inched back behind Pete.

"Maybe some of you can swim already," Cutter said, looking them up and down as though he could pick a swimmer out by sight. He pointed to a wooden raft floating several yards from the dock. "Think any of you can make it to the raft?"

Only Tonya and Tex raised their hands.

Billy gave Danny a jab. "You're *Jaws*, remember?" he whispered.

Danny's hand shot up.

"Terrific," Cutter said. "Let's start with you three. Everyone else can watch while we swim to the raft together. Pete and I will swim beside you. Okay, jump in."

Tex quietly slipped into the water.

In one quick movement, Tonya dropped her beach towel and jumped in with a big splash. Cold water washed onto the dock and over everyone's feet.

"Tidal Wave Tonya," one of the boys whispered.

Cutter shot him a warning look. "Watch it, mister. We're a team on my waterfront." He turned to Danny. "Jump in, son."

"I've mot a nold," Danny said.

"What did he say?" Cutter asked.

"He's got a cold," Pete explained, handing him Nurse Mudge's note.

Cutter read the note and shook his head. "Tough break, kiddo. Looks like you're land-locked for a few days. But don't worry. We'll have you in the water before the Camp Kick-apoo Water Races in two weeks."

Danny gulped. "Yes, sir."

Cutter gave Tex and Tonya last-minute instructions. "If either of you gets tired, grab on to Pete or me. We'll be alongside you."

Danny squeezed through some kids at the end of the dock to get a good view. Tonya and Tex pushed off. The girls cheered Tonya, while the boys chanted Tex's name.

Tex made swimming look like hard work. His arms and legs thrashed in the water. He had to grab on to Cutter twice to catch his breath.

But Tonya made swimming look easy. She kept a smooth, steady stroke. When she climbed onto the raft, the girls clapped.

The boys were quiet.

"She's okay," Billy had to admit.

Noah whipped his towel playfully at Danny. "Wait till our Jaws here gets rid of his cold. You'll show those girls. Right, Dan?"

Danny smiled weakly. "Sure. They don't call me *Jaws* for nothing." But he couldn't take his eyes from Tonya as she swam effortlessly back to the dock. She was really good.

"Okay, let's get the rest of you tadpoles swimming," Cutter said.

Danny watched from the dock as everyone waded into the lake up to their waists. Cutter soon had them floating on their backs.

Sweat trickled down Danny's face. *That*

water must feel cool, he thought. He sat down and dangled his feet in the water.

Just then, Billy waved to get his attention. "Did you see me float?" he yelled.

Danny stood on the edge of the dock and waved back so hard that he lost his balance. His arms circled, but he lurched forward.

"*Whoa-a-a!*" he screamed as he splashed into the water. In a panic, he tried to touch the lake bottom, but his feet slipped out from under him. Then he opened his mouth to call for help, but water rushed in. Gulping and thrashing, he felt himself going under.

Suddenly, a powerful

arm reached around his chest. "Relax, I've got you." It was Cutter. He pulled Danny up against him and held him until Danny found his footing on the lake's bottom.

A crowd quickly formed around them.

"Wow, he almost drowned," a boy said.

Billy waded over to Danny and put a hand on his shoulder. "Good one, Biggs. You had us fooled." He gave Danny a wink.

Cutter glared at Danny. "Was this a prank?"

Danny looked at Cutter's angry face. All he had to do was say "No" and he wouldn't be in trouble. But then all the kids would know he wasn't really a champion swimmer.

"I told you he was a big liar," Tonya said, loud enough for everyone to hear.

Then Danny knew what he had to do. He smiled and took a bow. He waved at the kids on the shore as if his gulping and thrashing had all been a big performance. Some of the kids started to applaud. They stopped when they saw Cutter's face.

"Drowning is no laughing matter, mister," Cutter said to Danny. "Until further notice, you are not allowed on my waterfront." He looked over his shoulder at Tonya.

"Young lady, you're an ace swimmer, but I don't much like your attitude. For the next week, you two will spend this time together working on your canoeing skills."

Danny's eyes locked with Tonya's. He watched as she took a finger and slowly drew it across her neck like a knife.

Billy whispered in Danny's ear, "I guess she didn't like your fat jokes."

Later that day during Rest Hour, the Muskies were on their bunks, reading or writing home.

Danny wrote a note to his parents:

Dear Mom and Dad,

    Come and get me quick. My life is in danger. If you can't find me, my body's at the bottom of Kickapoo Lake.

Your son,

    Danny

P.S. Tonya did it.

P.P.S. You should have taught me to swim.

[6]

Turtle Island, Help!

Danny stared at the eggs on his plate. He was too nervous to eat any breakfast.

For the past week Pete had been teaching Tonya and him how to canoe. This morning Pete was sending them out on the lake alone.

Billy waved a piece of bacon at Danny. "Come on, eat. You need your strength."

Danny shook his head. "If I eat, I'll just sink faster when Tonya shoves me overboard."

After breakfast, Danny saw Tonya waiting for him by the dock. She seemed bigger and scarier than usual. In her puffy red life jacket, she looked like a giant fire hydrant.

"You're late, Biggs," she snapped.

"Sorry." Danny slipped on his life jacket. *If I'm wearing this, they'll at least find my body,* he thought.

"Get in," Tonya ordered, handing him a

paddle. "You take the bow. We'll switch on the way back from Turtle Island."

Danny climbed into the front of the canoe. *Maybe if I shut up, she'll let me live.* He felt the canoe sink a little as Tonya stepped inside and sat in back. He felt her watching him. Was she plotting his murder?

"Paddle!" she shouted, pushing off.

Danny flinched at the sound of her voice. He dipped his paddle in the water as Tonya steered them toward Turtle Island.

"My counselor says Turtle Island used to be an Indian burial ground," Tonya said.

A burial ground! Danny's mind raced. *She's waiting till we're in the middle of the lake to clobber me with her paddle. Then she'll bury me on the island.*

Soon they were far from land. The people on shore looked like colored dots.

Sweat trickled down Danny's pale face.

"You seem weird, Biggs. What's wrong?"

"Nothing," Danny mumbled.

"For a big mouth, you're pretty quiet. Sure you don't have any more fat jokes?"

Danny laughed nervously. He was so rattled he started to hiccup.

Tonya sighed. "Swell. Now I have to listen to you hiccup. Try holding your breath."

Danny tried, but it didn't work.

"I know what'll get rid of them." Tonya began rocking the canoe back and forth.

Danny gripped the sides so tightly his knuckles turned white. "Stop!" he pleaded.

"No. This'll cure your hiccups," Tonya said, rocking harder.

Water splashed over the sides, and Danny began to lose his balance. He sank to the canoe's floor and clung to the seat. "Stop it!"

But Tonya just rocked the canoe harder. "What's wrong, *Jaws*? Afraid of the water?"

"No!" he answered.

"No? Are you sure?" Tonya threw the whole weight of her body from side to side. The canoe started to roll over.

"Stop!" Danny cried. "I can't swim!"

Suddenly the canoe was still. "I knew it," Tonya said. "You *are* a big liar."

Danny was very quiet as they both began to paddle again. *She didn't want to kill me*, he realized. *She just wanted me to admit I couldn't swim.*

As soon as they reached the island, Danny jumped out of the canoe and ran way up on shore. He wasn't taking any chances.

Tonya pulled the canoe onto the beach.

She spread out a towel on the sand. "I'm going for a swim!" she called to him.

Danny waited until she was in the water. Then he crept closer, ready to grab the canoe and escape. That's when he noticed some fruit sitting on her towel. He'd skipped breakfast and was now pretty hungry.

"I'll just have a snack first," he mumbled, grabbing a peach and sitting down. As he ate the juicy fruit, he noticed Tonya swimming back and forth along the shoreline.

Tonya rolled onto her back and did a flutter kick. One at a time, her arms circled up and down like a graceful windmill.

Danny tried to remember which stroke it was from his library book. "What's that called?" he finally shouted.

"The backstroke!" Tonya answered.

As Danny ate the rest of her fruit, Tonya called out the names of the different swimming strokes—sidestroke, breaststroke, and crawl.

"Look! I'm a dolphin!" she shouted, diving into the waves headfirst.

But Danny thought she looked more like a mermaid with her pretty yellow hair floating around her in the water.

"Watch this!" Floating on her back, Tonya lifted one leg straight up into the air. Then she slowly sank beneath the surface until only her toes were showing. She shot up out of the water, a big smile on her face. "That was water ballet!" she shouted.

Even her voice sounds happier in the water, thought Danny. He clapped his hands and waited to see what she would do next.

Tonya kicked both legs straight up into the air for an underwater handstand!

Suddenly, Danny understood why Tonya loved the water as much as he was afraid of it. In the water, Two Ton Tonya disappeared, and she became light as a feather. She wasn't a fat girl anymore. She was a water ballerina, a mermaid, a dolphin.

When Tonya came out of the lake, Danny could hardly believe she was the same girl. Water streamed down her heavy arms and legs.

She saw two peach pits and a banana peel on her towel. "Guess you were hungry."

"Sorry." Danny's stomach tightened as he waited for her to turn back into Two Ton Tonya. But she didn't.

"That's okay," she said, sitting beside him on the towel. "I'm supposed to be on a diet anyway." She hugged her legs and tried to cover her body.

Danny could tell she was embarrassed by her size. For the first time, he felt like saying something nice to her. "You know, you looked like a mermaid out there."

"Really?" Tonya couldn't hide the pleasure in her voice.

Danny nodded.

Tonya looked away. "Sometimes I wish I could live in the water."

"Not me," Danny piped up. "I'd sink." He gave her a playful nudge. "That's a joke. You're supposed to laugh."

Tonya gave a little chuckle.

They sat quietly for a long time just looking at the lake. Then Tonya said something so softly Danny had to lean forward to hear.

"I could teach you to swim," she said. "I mean, here on the island so no one knows."

"Really?"

Tonya gestured for Danny to follow as she walked waist-deep into the lake. "Let's start with floating. Watch me."

Tonya lay back on top of the water. Her arms and legs bobbed up and down on the gentle waves. Her yellow hair swirled around her smiling face. She made it look so easy. "Now you try," she said, standing up.

Danny held his breath and fell back into the water, stiff as a board. A small wave hit his face and he panicked. He felt himself sinking. He stood up quickly, sputtering water. "What did I do wrong?"

There was a smile on Tonya's face. But she didn't laugh at him. "You're trying too hard," she said. "Just relax. Let the water do the work. If you let your body go limp, the water will buoy you up. Come on. I'll help this time. Just lean back across my arms."

Danny was a little afraid to try again. But

he didn't want Tonya to think he was chicken. He slowly leaned back.

Tonya held her arms under his back until he was floating on top of the water. "Good," she said. "Arch your back more. That's it."

When Tonya started clapping, Danny realized she had removed her arms. He was floating all by himself!

After Danny tried floating a few more times, Tonya said, "We better head back."

They packed up to go, and Danny thought about how much fun Tonya was when she wasn't being a bully. He couldn't help asking, "Why aren't you nice like this all the time?"

"Guess," she said, looking down at her large body. "If I'm not mean first, kids make fun of me."

Danny felt guilty. He had made more fat jokes than anyone. He tried to think of something nice to say. "Nobody's perfect. Besides, you're a fantastic swimmer. I'm not really good at anything like you are."

"Thanks," said Tonya, handing him a paddle. "Is that why you brag all the time?"

Danny shrugged. "I guess so," he mumbled. "I mean, no one would like me if I didn't."

Tonya shook her head. "Billy would...and I would, too."

Danny glanced up to see if she was kidding him. But she wasn't. She really meant it.

When they got back to the dock, Billy was waiting for Danny. "Did she try to kill you?" he whispered.

"Not really," Danny said. "She's okay." He waved to Tonya as she left.

Billy gave Danny a puzzled look. But he seemed to have something more pressing on his mind. "I've got bad news," he said, shoving a piece of paper in front of Danny.

CAMP KICKAPOO WATER RACES
sign-up sheet
(Every camper must participate.)

relay: Noah, Tex, Billy, Danny (Jaws)

breaststroke: Tonya, Stacey, Matt, Jimmy

backstroke...

Billy pointed to Danny's name. "I tried to stop Noah, but he signed you up."

Danny pushed away the sheet. "I've got an excuse from Nurse Mudge. Remember?"

"No one has a cold for two weeks. Someone might get suspicious."

Maybe Billy's right, thought Danny.

At dinner that night in the Mess Hall, Danny took Tonya aside. "Can you teach me to swim in time for the water races next week?"

Tonya shook her head. "You can't learn any stroke that fast…except maybe one."

"I'll do it," Danny said. He was desperate. "Which stroke is it?"

Tonya couldn't help answering with a grin. "The dog paddle."

[7]

Dog-Paddle Danny

The day of the Camp Kickapoo Water Races finally arrived. Mr. Mike, the camp director, blasted the campers awake with his loud-speaker.

"Wake up, sleepyheads! Today's the day! Grab some breakfast and head to the water-front! Right, Luther?"

Mr. Mike's dog barked through the loud-speaker. Everyone covered their ears, laugh-ing—except Danny.

Tonya had tried her best to teach him to swim in time for the races, but he was lousy at it. Danny patted his survival kit, hidden under his sheet. It was his only hope.

He grabbed the kit and hurried toward the latrine so fast he tripped. Everything fell onto the ground.

Before he could stuff it all back inside his

bag, someone reached down and picked up his tube of fake boogers.

Danny looked up at Pete's scowling face.

"The jig's up, Jaws."

At breakfast, Danny was so miserable he couldn't eat a bite.

Noah had a second helping of eggs.

"Hey, Noah, stop pigging out," Tex said. "You'll slow us down in the relay."

Noah stuffed a piece of bacon in his mouth. "What are you worried about? We've got Jaws on our team. We can't lose."

Danny's stomach tightened. "I've been meaning to tell you guys. I'm not *that* good."

Noah grinned in admiration. "A champion swimmer, *and* he's modest. What a guy."

The Muskies nodded in agreement as they all reached over to give him a pat on the back.

Danny forced a smile. He couldn't wait for this day to end.

After breakfast, all the boys and girls hurried down to the waterfront. A bright-colored banner was strung over the dock. The Camp Kickapoo flag snapped in the wind.

"Look! The camp mascot!" Billy pointed to an inflatable kangaroo floating on the lake.

Cutter stood on the lifeguard chair and blew his whistle. Everyone was quiet.

"Welcome to the Camp Kickapoo Water Races! This morning we'll start with competitions in sailing, kayaking, and canoeing. Swimming events will be this afternoon!"

Danny had only four more hours to think of a way to get out of the races!

After lunch, Danny found Tonya waiting for him outside the Mess Hall. "I have an idea that might help," she whispered.

Danny was all ears as he listened to Tonya's plan.

Danny's relay was the last race of the day. The whole camp showed up for the event, including Nurse Mudge, all the counselors, Mr. Mike, and his dog, Luther.

Danny stood on the dock with his relay

teammates, Noah, Billy, and Tex.

"Which stroke are you going to swim?" Noah asked Danny. Since it was a beginners' event, the swimmers were allowed to choose.

"Dog paddle," Danny said loudly.

"What?" Noah looked worried.

"He's just kidding," Tex said.

"No, I'm not," Danny insisted. "I'm Dog-Paddle Danny. Right, Luther?" Danny barked like a dog until Luther ran onto the dock, jumping up and barking at him. Everyone was laughing until Cutter stood up on the lifeguard chair to announce their event.

"As you all know, the relay race is the last event of the day. Each member on the four-person team will swim to the opposite dock and back. Swimmers, take your mark."

Noah was up first. He gripped the edge of the dock with his toes.

"Get set!"

He bent at the waist, ready to dive in.

Cutter blew the whistle. Noah and three other swimmers dived in with a splash. Cheers rose up from the sidelines.

Noah kicked and splashed his way through the water in what looked like a mix of crawl, breaststroke, and butterfly.

Tex looked puzzled. "What stroke is *that?*"

"Who cares?" Billy grinned, jumping up and down. "He's way ahead!"

The instant Noah's hand touched the dock, Tex dived over his head into the water. He started a slow crawl stroke. *Very* slow.

Noah shook his head as he watched the other teams swim past Tex. "Now I know why it's called the crawl," he said.

By the time Tex made it back, they were in last place.

Billy was next. He started in the water, pushing off from the dock into a backstroke.

"Boy, this sure is a goofy race," Tex said, watching one of the swimmers change strokes for the third time. Another swimmer got so tired that he gave up and *walked* out of the lake.

"You're next," Noah said to Danny. "Eat 'em alive, Jaws."

But Danny was busy searching the crowd for Tonya. She stepped forward and gave him a thumbs-up sign. Then she went into action.

"Let's hear it for the amazing Dog-Paddle Danny!" she shouted as if presenting a circus act.

Danny barked and pretended to beg like a dog. Some of the other swimmers pointed at him and snickered.

"Hey, what's going on?" Noah asked.

Tex squinted at Danny through his glasses as if he couldn't believe his eyes.

The next thing they knew, Billy had finished, and Danny jumped into the lake doing the dog paddle. Luther stood on the edge of the dock barking at him.

Tex and Noah just stared at their dog-paddling bunkmate and the barking dog. Billy was bent over laughing.

Suddenly, Danny turned his head and barked back at Luther.

"Look!" A camper pointed as Luther took a flying leap off the dock and landed with a splash in the water. He began furiously dog-

paddling after Danny.

The entire camp roared with laughter. Even Cutter. No one was watching to see who was winning the relay anymore. All eyes were on Danny and Luther dog-paddling back to the dock.

Everyone was still laughing when Danny finished. But instead of being embarrassed,

Danny got out of the water and took a bow. Luther swam back to Mr. Mike. He shook his wet coat all over the surprised camp director.

The only ones who weren't laughing were Danny's teammates.

"We came in third place because of you," Noah said. "Why didn't you swim fast?"

Danny looked at their disappointed faces. "Sorry, but Tonya was right. I *am* Dog-Paddle Danny. 'Jaws' was just a story I made up."

"What a phony," Matt said, turning away.

"Yeah," Jimmy agreed. "You lied to us."

"Come on, guys," Billy said. "It was just a joke. You've got to admit it was funny."

Pete had been listening quietly. He spoke to the boys as they left Danny on the dock. "Don't be so hard on him. Danny was wrong to lead you on about being a good swimmer. But the Camp Kickapoo Water Races are about having fun, not winning. And no one made us laugh more than Danny. Right?"

"He *was* pretty funny," Jimmy admitted.

The other boys nodded in agreement.

Before they left the waterfront, one of

the counselors made an announcement. "Some of you haven't picked up your Arts and Crafts projects. This is my *last* warning."

Mr. Mike stepped forward. "And don't forget tonight's special campfire by the lake!"

Some of the campers gave a tired cheer.

The Muskies decided to stop by the Arts and Crafts cabin together on their way back to South Camp. They shared their finished projects with each other.

Tex had sewn a leather eyeglass case and painted a picture of his horse, Sailor, on it. Noah slipped on a T-shirt he had tie-dyed in bright colors. Matt and Jimmy had made candles with pine cones and leaves inside.

Everyone agreed Billy's project was the coolest. He had woven multi-colored friendship bracelets for all the Muskies.

"You have to wear them till they rot off," Billy said.

"I already picked up my project," Danny lied. "It's back at the tent." But it was really stuck in his back jeans pocket.

When Danny stepped outside the Arts

and Crafts cabin, he found Tonya there waiting for him.

"I made this for you to write your stories in," she said, holding out a funny-looking notebook. Strips of bark covered both sides. She pointed to a small twig glued to the front cover. "That's me," she said shyly.

"Thanks." Danny didn't know what else to say. He reached into his back pocket and pulled out a big plastic comb covered with tiny shells and sparkles. "This is for you. It's a mermaid comb," he explained.

Tonya's face lit up. "It's beautiful."

"See you later." Danny ran to catch up with his friends. When he turned to wave good-bye, Tonya was already using the comb. Sparkles glittered through her yellow hair. She looked just like a real mermaid.

That night, the Muskies stayed up late telling ghost stories until Pete stopped by.

"Lights out, Muskies," Pete said, turning out the lantern. As soon as he left, someone shouted, "Bite count!"

Danny immediately started counting all the mosquito bites on his arms and legs.

"Ten," Tex said with disappointment.

"Twelve," Jimmy piped up.

"Fifteen," Matt said. "If Jimmy and I add ours together, it's twenty-seven. We win!"

"No way," everyone protested.

"I've got thirty-two," Noah said.

Danny was still counting.

"Twenty-five," Billy said.

Danny waited until it was quiet. "Fifty-one," he said with pride.

Noah moaned. Billy kicked the bottom of Danny's bunk with his foot. "You win."

Danny smiled and scratched both legs. *Camp is great!* he thought. Then he reached under his pillow for his flashlight. He flipped open his new notebook and wrote the title of his first story at the top of the page.

The Mermaid of Turtle Island
by Danny Biggs

About the Author

A veteran camper, Gibbs Davis canoed over one hundred miles to the Mississippi River and had more sunburns and mosquito bites than anyone else in her tent. (Her big sister Bronwen's camp nickname was Twig.)

Since her camp days, Gibbs Davis has had twenty books for young readers published.

Gibbs warns not to try reading in the bathtub. "People swim," she notes. "Books sink."

¤ ¤ ¤

About the Illustrator

Abby Carter is the talented illustrator of several books for children including the best-selling *Great-Uncle Dracula* and *Baseball Ballerina*. She lives in Maine.